THE MASK™
THE ANIMATED SERIES

THE MASK FOR MAYOR!

Adapted by Nancy E. Krulik
Based on the television script by Dean Stefan
Illustrated by Aristides Ruiz

SCHOLASTIC INC.
New York Toronto London Auckland Sydney

ISBN 0-590-50206-9

12 11 10 9 8 7 6 5 4 3 2 1   6 7 8 9/9 0 1/0

Printed in the U.S.A.   24

First Scholastic printing, January 1996

Stanley Ipkiss was having a bad day. Already he had stepped in garbage, had his money stolen, received a parking ticket — and it wasn't even lunchtime! No doubt about it, things had gotten really bad in Edge City!

"I'll tell ya one thing," Stanley said to his dog, Milo. "If I were mayor, things would be different." Stanley kicked at the garbage by his feet. "Yeah, right," he mumbled, "like I could ever be mayor."

Then a crazy, toothy grin flashed across his face. Maybe Stanley couldn't be mayor, but he *could* give him a piece of his mind. With a little help from *The Mask!*

Stanley raced home and headed for his closet. That's where he kept an ancient mask he'd found floating in the river. The mask had special powers. The minute Stanley put it on his face, he was transformed into The Mask — a wacky, green superhero. The Mask could do just about anything!

As soon as Stanley stepped into his closet, Milo dove under the bed in fear. He knew what was coming next!

Wind blasted. Music blared. Bright lights flashed. Then the closet door opened, and out stepped . . . The Mask!

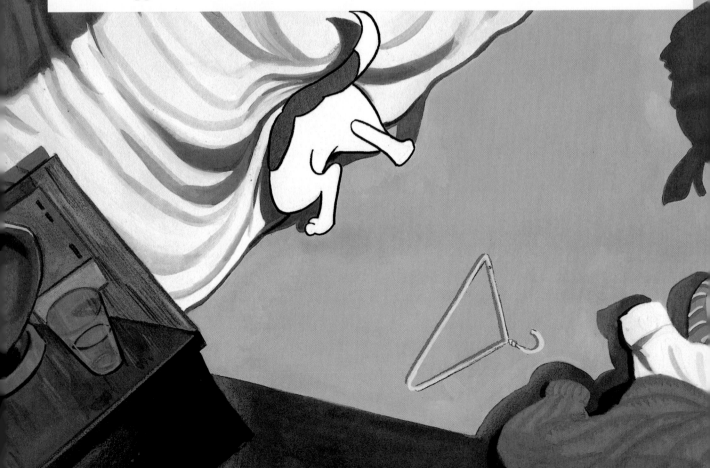

Unfortunately, the whole fight was recorded by the news cameras. On the evening news, it looked like The Mask had beaten up Mayor Tilton. After all, Stanley was the only one who knew that Mayor Tilton was really Pretorius! To everyone else, it looked like *The Mask* was the bad guy.

Pretorius smiled as he watched the news. "The Mask is on his way to losing the election," he bellowed. "Edge City will soon be mine!"

The Mask's first stop was a press conference where Mayor Tilton was unveiling a statue — of himself. The mayor was in for a huge surprise. When he yanked the curtain off the statue, Mayor Tilton came face-to-face with . . . The Mask!? "Speaking on behalf of all the pigeons in the city," The Mask said with a laugh, "I just wanna say, great statue!"

The Mask zoomed around the city, taking his campaign promises straight to the people.

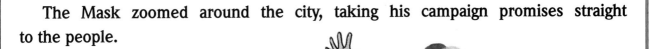

"I've decided to throw my hat into the ring as mayor," he announced to the cheering crowd.

"Yes, friends, vote for me, the guy who invented the green party!" he continued.

"I'm the original party animal! Hee haw, hee haw."

The Mask campaigned late into the night. The next morning, Stanley was very tired. Stanley couldn't remember what The Mask had been up to. But he found out soon enough!

"And now the news," the radio announcer said. "The newest candidate to enter the mayoral race is . . . The Mask!"

Stanley gulped. "He is? I mean, I am?"

This time, The Mask had gotten Stanley into really big trouble!

"This is terrible, Milo," Stanley cried. "The Mask can't run this city. He's got too many weird ideas. I can just see him turning city council meetings into limbo parties. And worse!"

Stanley had to stop him! He picked up the old mask and handed it to the dog. "Milo, when I go to work this morning, I want you to hide the mask," he ordered. "You've got to promise that under no circumstances, no matter how much I beg or plead, you will NOT give me the mask!"

That evening, on his way home from work, Stanley saw something very unusual. Two garbagemen were actually picking up garbage!

"About time you guys started picking up the trash," Stanley told them.

The garbagemen grabbed Stanley and lifted him off the ground like yesterday's trash.

"Mr. Ipkiss," one garbageman snarled, "if you'd be good enough to accompany us, the mayor would like to see you."

Stanley didn't exactly have a choice. The garbagemen carried him all the way to City Hall. Stanley's knees shook as he heard Mayor Tilton's loud footsteps *click-clack* down the long, dark hall.

"You wanted to see me, Mr. Mayor?" Stanley asked nervously.

Mayor Tilton gave him a menacing grin. "That's right. I do want to see you . . . DEAD!"

Stanley bolted down the hallway! "This is too weird," Stanley said to no one in particular. "What's got into Mayor Tilton?"

"Funny you should ask," the mayor replied, emerging from the shadows. He ripped open his shirt — and his chest — to reveal a huge, hideous head!

Stanley stared. This wasn't Mayor Tilton. This was Pretorius, the evilest evildoer in all of Edge City! Pretorius was a very busy bad guy; so busy he had to divide himself in two. That way his head could carry out one crime, while his body carried out another.

Stanley was in MAJOR trouble!

Pretorius described his dastardly plan. He was going to convince everyone he was Mayor Tilton. Then, once the "mayor" was reelected, Pretorius would turn Edge City into a giant toxic waste dump. As if that weren't bad enough, Pretorius had discovered a special toxic chemical that would turn its victims into mutant slaves.

"And you, Mr. Ipkiss," Pretorius snarled. He picked up a test tube filled with a putrid, bubbling liquid. "You will be my first human guinea pig for toxic waste subvariety 57-B!"

Stanley knocked over a table and made a run for it!

Stanley dashed into his apartment and locked the door behind him. But Pretorius wasn't far behind. There was only one way Stanley could survive.

"Milo, you've gotta tell me where you hid the mask," Stanley pleaded. But the dog wouldn't show him. After all, Stanley had made him promise not to.

"Okay, I'll find it myself," Stanley said. He frantically scanned the room. "There's an awful lot of food in Milo's bowl," he thought out loud.

The mask was in Milo's dog-food bowl!

"Did you really think you could escape me, Mr. Ipkiss?" Pretorius asked, bursting into the room. "After all, you can't fight City Hall."

Phhzzt! Pretorius pulled out a stun gun and zapped Stanley.

"EEYOUCH!" Stanley screamed. He tumbled backwards — and right out the window.

Stanley seemed done for. And he should have been. Except that now Stanley was The Mask! And remember, The Mask can do just about anything.

Even when he's running for his life, a good mayoral candidate always stops to talk to news reporters.

"Interview? I'd love to," The Mask told one reporter. "But first, ma'am, if you'll excuse me, I've gotta deal with a dirty, lowdown varmint." Then he turned and walked back into his apartment building.

The Mask and Pretorius met up in the lobby. With a flick of his wrist, The Mask lifted the rug right out from under Pretorius. Pretorius flipped into the air and landed with a thud!

Pretorius struggled to his feet. But The Mask was too fast for him. He body-slammed him back down to the ground.

Back at his apartment, Stanley was watching the same news program. But he wasn't doing much smiling.

"And here I thought The Mask as mayor would be bad news," he moaned. "But this is worse. Pretorius is going to win the election and turn Edge City into a toxic waste dump. As much as it makes my skin crawl, we have to get The Mask back into the race."

The election was coming up fast. There wasn't much time. Both candidates had very busy schedules.

While Pretorius, disguised as Mayor Tilton, was out campaigning for his political party,

The Mask was planning limbo parties.
"Somebody *stop* me!" he joked.

The phony Mayor Tilton spent his day pressing flesh.

The Mask spent *his* day pressing trousers. "I'm smokiiiin'!" he cried out to the crowd.

By the time election day arrived, the race was too close to call. Stanley and Milo spent the day in front of the TV. Just for luck, Stanley crossed his fingers, arms, legs, and feet.

"This just in," the newscaster said. "We can now declare a winner — The Mask wins, by one vote!"

Stanley leaped up and hugged Milo. "Yes!" he exclaimed. "The Mask is the winner." Then Stanley's face fell. "Which means the life of Stanley Ipkiss as he knows it is about to come to a screeching halt." Stanley took a deep breath. "I can't think about that now."

Stanley went into his closet as a private citizen. He came out as Mayor Mask!

The Mask raced over to Mayor Tilton's campaign headquarters and took the stage.

"I'd like to take this opportunity to begin my term in office with a proverbial BANG!" he said, pulling a lit bomb from his jacket.

The Mask threw the bomb right at the fake Mayor Tilton's chest.

Pretorius's head burst free and shot out into the crowd!

"I may have lost the election," Pretorius's head shouted, "but I am still going through with making Edge City Harbor the world's largest toxic waste dump. My 'other half' is at this very moment about to release toxic ooze from the first barge."

The Mask just smiled. "Unless I beat him to it, brainpan," he said.

Pretorius may have had the last word — who knows? No one could hear him over the noise of the Mask Chopper's revving engine.

The Mask spotted Pretorius's headless body waterskiing its way over to the barge. "Yoo hoo!" The Mask called to him. "Tall, dark, and headless!"

Pretorius's body felt a tug on his water ski. The Mask had tied his towline to Pretorius's leg!

Pretorius's body might have been brainless, but it wasn't stupid. The body stopped dead, launching The Mask high into the air.

It didn't take long for The Mask to get back on track. He raced after Pretorius's body, trying to stop it before it reached the barge.

Oof! A speeding torpedo rammed into The Mask's back! And this was no run-of-the-mill torpedo! *This* torpedo carried Pretorius's head.

The Mask smashed into a pool of green, toxic slime! Yuck!

"How ironic," Pretorius snickered. "Destroyed by the very toxic ooze he was fighting so valiantly against!"

But it takes more than toxic slime to destroy The Mask! In fact, The Mask emerged from the green gook stronger than ever. He was ready to . . . play football! The Mask grabbed Pretorius's head and punted him high into the air. The head got stuck on a jumbo jet that was flying by.

"And it's good!" The Mask cried out. "That head is heading nonstop to Hawaii!"

But there was still the matter of Pretorius's headless body to take care of. Quickly, The Mask placed a high-powered turbo engine on one of the body's water skis. Pretorius's body zoomed off, destined for parts unknown!

"When you hit Australia, drop me a postcard," The Mask cried after the speeding body.

That was the end of the fake Mayor Tilton. But where was the *real* Mayor Tilton?

A TV reporter discovered him tied up in a lifeboat in the river. "How does it feel to lose the election by one vote?" she asked him.

"I didn't," Mayor Tilton replied. "I never got to vote. And I've still got five minutes until the polls close."

The mayor hurried off to vote for himself. Now the race for mayor was tied. That is, until Stanley Ipkiss arrived. *He* hadn't gotten a chance to vote, either.

"Vote for me. I'll give you anything," Mayor Tilton begged Stanley.

Stanley whispered something in his ear. Mayor Tilton nodded. "Limbo parties," the mayor assured him.

That settled it. Stanley cast his vote for Mayor Tilton.

So much for Mayor Mask!